a minedition book published by Penguin Young Readers Group

For Colin, JG

Text and illustrations copyright © 2006 by Julia Goschke

Coproduction with Michael Neugebauer Publishing Ltd., Hong Kong.

Rights arranged with "minedition" Rights and Licensing AG, Zurich, Switzerland.

Published simultaneously in Canada.

Manufactured in Hong Kong by Wide World Ltd.

Typesetting in Baskerville Old Face

Library of Congress Cataloging-in-Publication Data available upon request.

ISBN 0-698-40038-0

10 9 8 7 6 5 4 3 2 1

First Impression

For more information please visit our website: www.minedition.com

Julia Goschke

Langley Longears

Translated by Charise Myngheer

Langley woke up to a bright new day.

"Come on! Let's play catch!" called his brothers and sisters.

Langley jumped up and started running. But then... *Boom!*

He tripped and landed on his nose.

The other puppies laughed at him, and poor Langley sulked.

"Maybe we should play hide-and-seek instead," suggested one puppy. "One, two, three..."

Quickly, Langley hid behind the fence. "...Nine, ten! Here I come, ready or not!"

But Langley's long ears were so easy to spot that he was tagged immediately.

"With those ears, you don't have a chance," laughed the puppies.

Langley didn't think they were funny.

"These stupid ears!" thought Langley.

"Why am I the only one with oversized ears?"

Again and again Langley tried to make his ears look smaller.

He tried pinning them up, wrapping them around and even tucking them in, but nothing really worked.

Frustrated, Langley gave up.

He curled up in the dog house and went to sleep.

When Langley woke up, the meadow was completely quiet.

"Helloooo, where are you?" he called. But his brothers and sisters were gone.

Langley went looking for them, but he didn't find them in the house either.

"If they're not here," thought Langley, "then they have to be in the forest."

Langley entered the forest nervously.

The thick trees hid the sun and made everything really dark.

"Hello, Rabbit," chirped something suddenly.

Langley jumped at the sound.

Above him was a little bird flapping its wings.

"I'm not a rabbit," said Langley. "I'm a dog!"

"Sorry!" chirped the bird. "Your ears are so long, I mistook you for someone else."

"Grrrr!" growled Langley, annoyed. But then he asked, "Hey, have you seen my brothers and sisters anywhere?"

"No," chirped the little bird, "I haven't seen any other dogs today.

Let's ask Rabbit. He seems to know everything that happens in the forest."

But Rabbit just shook his head. "Sorry, I haven't seen anyone today," he said, "but wouldn't you hear them if they were near?"

"What are you talking about?" asked Langley.

"Your ears. They're as big as mine. I use my big ears to hear things most others can't. Just perk them up like this," Rabbit said. "Then slowly turn them in different directions. Now you try it."

Langley tried to lift his ears to listen, but they wouldn't stay up, so the little bird helped hold them.

"Hey! I hear them! They're over there!" Langley shouted. "But they're howling and whimpering. Something terrible has happened. We have to find them!"

Langley shot off so quickly that Rabbit and the little bird almost couldn't keep up with him.

The howling began to get louder and—Whoa! They stopped suddenly.
They almost fell into the same deep hole where Langley's brothers and sisters were trapped.

"Whew!" said Langley. "That was close. Don't worry. I'll get you out!"
But how?
Langley clapped one of his long ears over his eyes so that he could think
more clearly. Then looking at his new friends, he said, "I've got it! I have
an idea that just might work. I need your help."
"No problem," they both answered.

"Heave-ho!"

Langley and his friends found a tree trunk and pushed it down into the deep hole. One puppy after another climbed out. Excitedly, the puppies surrounded their smart brother. "Wow! You saved us!" they cheered.

"I didn't think we'd ever get out," said one sister. "It was so dark," said the littlest one.

"And I was getting hungry!" complained Langley's bigger brother.

"The tree trunk was a great idea!" they all agreed. "Thank you, Langley. You're the best!"

The puppies had had enough of the forest for one day, so they headed back to the meadow to play with their new friends. They rolled around in the grass, as happy as can be. Then Rabbit looked up and saw that Langley was leaving, and he followed him.

Rabbit found Langley sitting in front of an old mirror trying to get his ears to stay up. "Hey Rabbit, is there a trick to this?" Langley asked hopelessly. "I thought maybe I had finally found something they were good for."

"Stop worrying," said his new friend. "You'll never be like a rabbit. You're a dog—the most outstanding dog around. Besides, it's what's between your ears that counts!"

Langley smiled for the first time all day.